BARFBURGER BABY, I WAS HERE FIRST

Paula Danziger

illustrated by

G. Brian Karas

G. P. Putnam's Sons   New York

For everyone who is an older brother or sister......

For everyone who is a younger brother or sister.....

Oh, okay......and for everyone who is an only child.

—P.D.

For my brother, Greg.

—G.B.K.

Text copyright © 2004 by Paula Danziger.
Illustrations copyright © 2004 by G. Brian Karas.
All rights reserved. This book, or parts thereof, may not be reproduced
in any form without permission in writing from the publisher,
G. P. Putnam's Sons, a division of Penguin Young Readers Group,
345 Hudson Street, New York, NY 10014. G. P. Putnam's Sons, Reg. U.S. Pat. & Tm. Off.
The scanning, uploading and distribution of this book via the Internet or via any other means
without the permission of the publisher is illegal and punishable by law.
Please purchase only authorized electronic editions, and do not participate in or encourage
electronic piracy of copyrighted materials. Your support of the author's rights is appreciated.
Published simultaneously in Canada. Manufactured in China by South China Printing Co. Ltd.
Designed by Gina DiMassi. Text set in Imperfect Regular. The art was done in gouache and acrylic with pencil.
Library of Congress Cataloging-in-Publication Data
Danziger, Paula, 1944– Barfburger baby, I was here first / Paula Danziger ; illustrated by G. Brian Karas.
p. cm. Summary: Five-year-old Jonathon is not pleased when neighbors and relatives come to visit
and admire his new baby brother. [1. Babies—Fiction. 2. Jealousy—Fiction. 3. Brothers—Fiction.]
I. Karas, G. Brian, ill. II. Title. PZ7.D2394Bar 2004 [E]—dc21 2003006472
ISBN 0-399-23204-4
10 9 8 7 6 5 4 3 2 1
First Impression

I sn't he the sweetest little baby brother?" Mom asks. She's making silly faces at Daniel.

Daniel has gunk all over his face. He looks like he spit up a space blob.

"He's just a Barfburger Baby," I whisper to myself.

"Jonathon Arthur Robinson, I heard that," Mom says. "Stop calling your brother Barfburger Baby."

"He likes being called that," I say. "Look. He's smiling."

"That's gas," she tells me.

"Gasburger Baby!" I grin.

"Jonathon Arthur Robinson," my mother says. "Not funny. No more names. Not now, not when company comes, not ever. You're Daniel's big brother."

I didn't ask to be the big brother.

I think one kid, ME, was just right. Kid number two, Daniel, just lies in his crib, drooling.

I just think, I'm glad I was here first.

Dad comes in and tickles Daniel. He giggles and gurgles.
I just stare and think, Barfburger Baby, Spaceblobburger,
Giggleburger Baby.

"Jonathon, honey, I know a baby brother takes some getting used to, but think of all the fun you're going to have when you two get older," Mom says.

I was here first. But I think about it.

We can play wagon train.

We can play pirates.

We can play spaceship.

We can play darts.

Mom and
Dad go downstairs
to wait for the company
coming to meet Barfburger Baby.
He just lies there, drooling and smelling like
he's doing other things . . . Poopburger Baby.

I start building a
giant wall of blocks between
me and Barfburger Baby.
"We're here!" It's Grandma Alice and Poppop. "We want to
see our new grandchild."
They have a big truck for me and a fuzzy duck for Daniel.

They make cooey
and gooey sounds at
Daniel. "Such a cutie! What a
lucky baby to have a big brother
to look after you!"

I just keep building my wall.

Grandma Alice carries Daniel downstairs and puts him in his
crib where everyone can see him.

"You are a good boy, my Jonathon Pookie Bear," Grandma says.
"I know that you will be a good big brother."

GRRRRR. . . . Grrrr to being a big brother and *Grrrr* to being called Jonathon Pookie Bear. I'm big now and everyone still calls me Jonathon Pookie Bear just because I called my bear "Winnie Pookie Bear" when I was little.

Our neighbors come in carrying plates of cookies.

"Hello, Jon Boy," Mrs. Peterson says.

"Your favorite," Mr. Peterson says.
"Butterscotch chip."

I'm glad Daniel doesn't
have any teeth to eat all
of my cookies.

Grandma Ruthie and Grandpa arrive.

"How are my boys?" Grandma Ruthie says.

They used to say, "How is our favorite only grandchild?"

Now they can't because of Daniel, Babyburger Baby.

They give Daniel
a mobile with cloth goldfish
and stuff hanging from it.
I think they should have
given him one with real
sharks hanging from it.

The grown-ups stand around Daniel, saying how cute he is.
Aunt Annie whispers, "You'll always be my Jonathon Pookie Bear."
"GRRRRRRRRRRR," I say, and crash my toy truck.

Aunt Annie goes over to Daniel.

Everyone is watching Mom change Daniel . . . Yuckburger.

Daniel sneezes . . . Sneezeburger. I hope that he sneezes
so hard that he covers everyone with his snot and stuff.
Snotburger Baby!

Uh-oh! My
cousins arrive.

"Jonathon Pookie Bear," my big cousin Charlie says,
punching me on the shoulder.

Holly and Polly, the twins, giggle and sing, "Jonathon
Pookie Bear has no hair . . . and he's bare!"

GRRRRR . . . double *GRRRRR.*

Aunt Patty says to Mom, "Remember when the twins were born . . . how unhappy Charlie was when they came home? Look at them now. They get along so much better. . . ."

I play with my Legos.

The twins start showing off.

First Daniel . . . now this . . . I wonder if a five-year-old can go to outer space and find a planet where there are no Barfburger Baby brothers and no annoying cousins. I will call it Jonathonland and be king.

Charlie comes over. "Jonathon Pookie Bear, what are you building?"

GRRRRR. . . . I ignore him.

Charlie looks at my town. "Hey, that's really good! I want to make something too." Charlie picks up a Lego.

I just keep building my racetrack.

"Please, Jonathon," Charlie says. "I won't
call you Pookie Bear ever again . . .
at least not for today."
He grins.

I think about it.
"Make a gas station," I say.

Charlie builds one, a really great one.

"All it needs now is gas," he says.

"Gasburger Baby has a lot of that.
We can just put a hose in him
and he can fill it up," I tell Charlie.

We laugh.

"Now that you're a big brother too, we should start a club.
The Big Brother Club. I'll be the president and you can be the
vice president."

Daniel sneezes . . . Sneezeburger Baby.

"Okay, Mr. President," I tell Charlie. "Just wait here a minute!"

I rush off and grab Winnie Pookie Bear. I give him to Daniel.
"Okay, Barfburger Baby, he's yours *for now*," I whisper.
"And when you get older, if we get along, I'll teach you to
say *GRRRRRRRRR*."

"Attention, everyone,"
I say, pointing at Daniel.
"Now he's Daniel Pookie Bear,
and I am Jonathon.
JUST Jonathon. And don't forget that!"

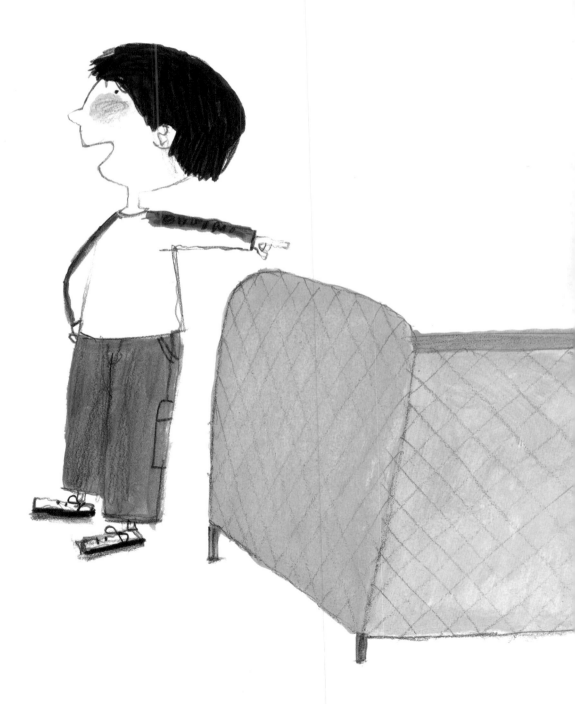

I go back to play.

"Hey, Jonathon! JUST Jonathon," Charlie says.

I don't even get mad. I just run my truck over his foot.